Sugar on SNOW

Also by Nancy Dingman Watson
Annie's Spending Spree

Sugar on SNOW

BY

Nancy Dingman Watson

ILLUSTRATIONS BY

Aldren A. Watson

New York · THE VIKING PRESS

Fourth printing November 1966
Pic Bk

First published in 1964 by The Viking Press, Inc.
625 Madison Avenue, New York, N.Y. 10022
Published simultaneously in Canada
by The Macmillan Company of Canada Limited
Library of Congress catalog card number: 64-21474
PRINTED IN THE U.S.A. BY HALLIDAY LITHOGRAPH CORP.

To Grandmommy
who gave Peter his first buckets
and to Big Shot
Norman McLeod Dingman
without whom nothing would have worked

"Sugar on snow,
Sugar on snow,
Pickles and doughnuts and
Sugar on snow!" sang Cammie.

"What's sugar on snow?" said Cait.

"You'll see on my birthday!
Sugar on snow,
Pickles and doughnuts and
Sugar on snow!" sang Cammie.

7

"Today is the day to tap the trees," said Peter, sniffing the air. "Tomorrow we boil the sap."

"Day after tomorrow
is my birthday!" chanted Cammie. "I'll invite
Meggie and Mary
and Johnny and Sverre
and Seth and Hannah and Arlo.
Just think, a sugar-on-snow party for my birthday!"

"But there is no sugar," said Cait,
"and there is no snow."

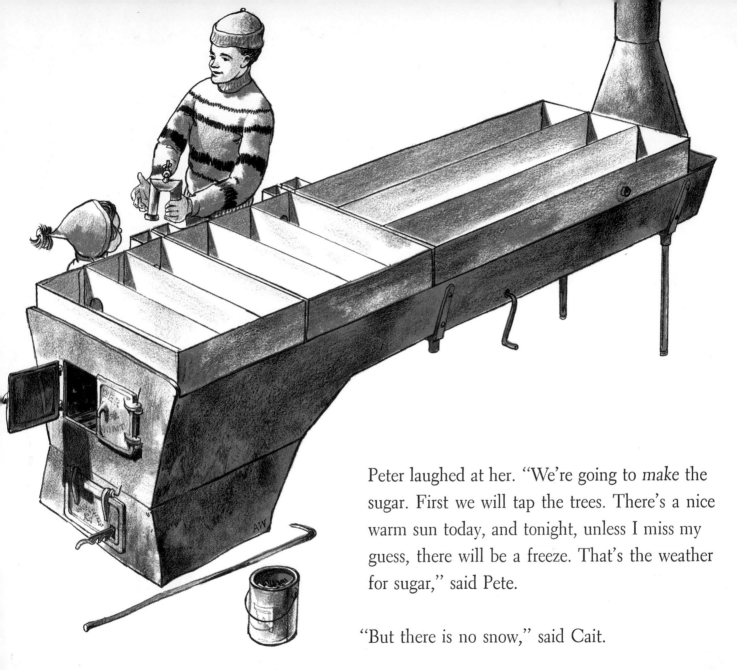

Peter laughed at her. "We're going to *make* the sugar. First we will tap the trees. There's a nice warm sun today, and tonight, unless I miss my guess, there will be a freeze. That's the weather for sugar," said Pete.

"But there is no snow," said Cait.

9

They climbed onto the wagon with the spouts and buckets and lids.
They jogged along the woods road with Leif and Reddy
and Frosty and Dick.

"Why didn't we sugar a week ago when there was plenty
of snow? Then we could have had sugar on snow easily,"
said Cammie.

"It wasn't your birthday then," said Cait.

"You can't just sugar whenever you want,"
  Peter said to Cam. "You wait until spring
  when the trees get warm
  and the sap begins to run."

"How do you know it isn't running
  if you don't even try?" asked Cait.

"Well," said Peter, "a farmer just knows. There's a different feel in the air.
In winter the earth is frozen tight, the trees creak with cold at night
and even the noonday sun doesn't melt the icicles
wrapped around the twigs.
Little animals stay huddled up from the cold, the birds don't sing,
and the sap stays down in the roots under the cold earth.

"Then one day it's sugaring time. The sun warms your cheek and the birds
begin to sing. Everything touched by the warm sun kind of stretches and begins
to feel alive again. That's when the sap rises in the maples."

"That's when you have to catch the sap—
    when it's cold from winter and sweet from spring.
    You sugar for a few weeks or maybe a month or so, and snap—
    it's over as quick as it began.
    Then the woods get a rosy pink flush
    and the buds swell into leaves,
    and sugaring is all over for another year."

13

Across the brook and through the woods they drove to the sugar bush.
A winter rabbit scurried away and a squirrel hid under the leaves.
The maple giants towered above and the woods were chill and peaceful.
But when they stopped the wagon to listen they heard birds' songs and
the beating of wings, the running of snow-cold rivulets of water over roots
to the brook, and the silence of clouds moving through the blue heavens.

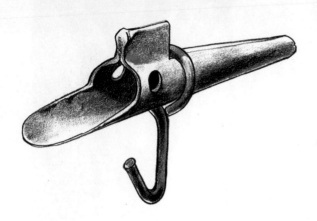

Peter took the brace and bit and made a hole
in the first bare tree. Snowy chips and silver
slivers sifted over his muddy boots.

Peter tapped a spout into the hole. Then he
stood back to watch. A bright, shiny drop of sap
rolled out and landed on Caitie's tongue.
"Yum-lish!" said Cait.

Cammie hung a bucket under the spout.
Caitie put on the lid.
The sap began to drip, drop—
bang, bang, bang! in the bucket.
Sugaring had begun.

Through the sugar bush they went, tapping the maple trees. Dick and Frosty pulled the load and Leif and Reddy ran behind chasing rabbits and barking at squirrels.

"We'll have sugar on snow for my birthday!" said Cam.

"If it snows," said Cait.

The sun went down, the shadows grew long, Daddy whistled from the house.
Over the meadow and through the woods the wagon banged
and rattled home.

Cammie and Peter fed Frosty and Dick, Caitie fed Leif and Red.
Mother fed everyone roast beef and apple pie and then it was time for bed.

Next morning they all went out, hitched up the horses and went to the woods.
Cammie jumped down and lifted a lid.

"The buckets are filled with crystal sap!
And they sparkle like little oceans in the sunlight!" she cried.

"Okay, pour it into the gathering tank," said Pete.

24

Caitie sat on the wagon and tugged at the horses' reins. Dick and Frosty didn't mind when Caitie struggled and tugged. They kept their ears pricked toward Peter to hear his "Giddup!" and "Whoa!"

When all the buckets were empty and hung back on the trees, Peter and Cammie and Cait drove home.

"Slosh-splash!" sang the sap in the tank.

Dick and Frosty hauled the sap up to the sugar house.
Into the storage tank it went and from there
through a pipe to the sugar pan.

26

Peter built a roaring fire in the sugar house arch.
Cammie and Caitlin carried wood, piles and piles
and *piles* of wood.

27

The sap got warm.

It got hot.

Little bubbles danced in the bottom of the pan.

The sap began to boil and jump.

Steam curled up to the ceiling.

It smelled like sugar, but it wasn't sugar yet.

All afternoon the sap tumbled and bubbled.
Cammie tasted it.
It tasted thin and golden and sweet.
But it wasn't syrup yet.

Caitie tasted it and tasted it.
It tasted hot and sticky
and it dribbled down her snowsuit
and the dribbles tasted like sugar.

The sugar house tasted like clouds
and it smelled steamy and mapley.
Outside it got dark and they had supper
of eggs boiled hard in the hot sap and the sap
was still boiling.
The fire roared like a hungry goblin.
It made Peter's face glow red
and it gobbled up all the wood
Cammie and Cait could carry.

The moon came out and it was clear and cold
and the stars had little twinkles of wings that sparkled.
Mother let them stay up late to boil,
because tomorrow was Cammie's birthday and
they *had* to have syrup for a sugar-on-snow party.

"Ho!" said Peter, when it was very late.

"Time to draw off."

He turned the spigot and out came *syrup*, all finished.

"SYRUP!" shouted Cammie.

"Syrup for my sugar-on-snow party!"

But Caitie said, "Huh, there is no snow."
Cammie blinked back tears.

Next morning Cammie jumped out of bed.
She flew to the window.
Would there be snow for her sugar-on-snow party?

"Happy birthday to Cammie!" shouted Peter and Cait.
"SNOW!" yelled Cammie.

A blanket of snow lay over the ground.
White cupcakes of snow sat on every fence post.
The bush by the kitchen door had long white fingers of snow
on every twig.
The barn and the sugar house had thick white snow icing on their roofs
like birthday cakes.
The meadow was smooth and twinkling with snow
just waiting for the first ski tracks to be sliced across it.

So they had the party.
Mother made fresh cinnamon doughnuts
and Daddy brought home rich red apple cider.

38

Down the road came all of Cammie's friends.
There were Meggie and Mary
and Johnny and Sverre
and Seth and Hannah and Arlo.
They raced for the sugar house.

Peter boiled syrup until it was
just right for sugar on snow.
Cammie and Caitlin made a smooth-packed place
in the nice clean snow.
Then Peter dribbled golden hot syrup over the packed place
and it got cold and waxy and chewy.

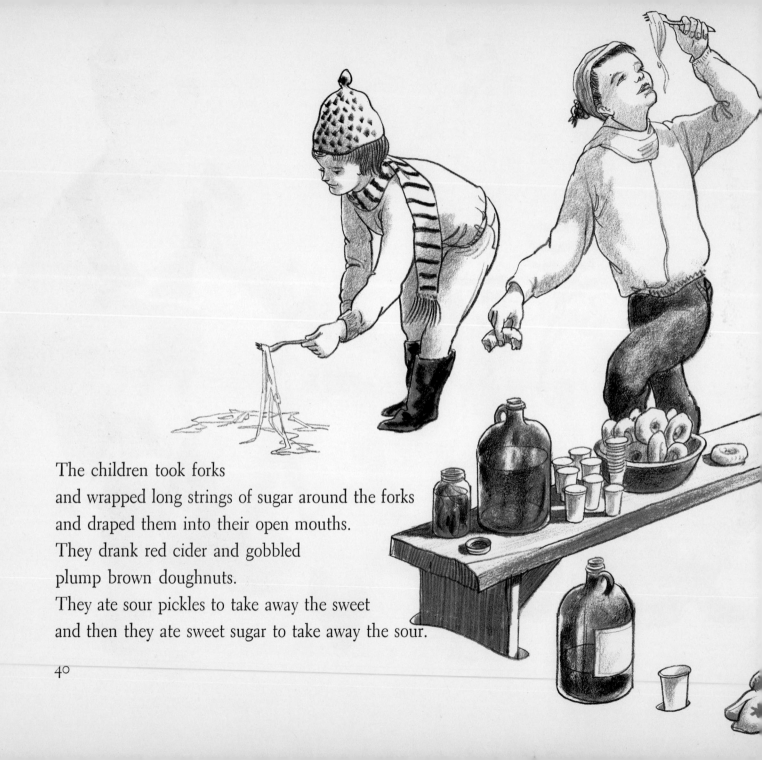

The children took forks
and wrapped long strings of sugar around the forks
and draped them into their open mouths.
They drank red cider and gobbled
plump brown doughnuts.
They ate sour pickles to take away the sweet
and then they ate sweet sugar to take away the sour.

They ate until they got silly.
Caitie stood on her head.

41

When the party was over
Peter and Dick and Frosty
took all the children home in the sled.

"Happy birthday, Cammie!" they called.
"Thank you for the sugar-on-snow party."

"Thank you for coming," said Cammie.

And Caitie said,
"It's lucky it snowed."

43